MOTEL ST. SIMON

A Horror Novella

BY E.V. DEAN

For Nuche

FIRST EDITION, MAY 2025
Copyright © 2025 E.V. Dean

Horror World Books
Los Angeles, California

CHAPTER 1

———◆———

"I believe I'm supposed to be upgraded with every stay?" she says as she hands the thick platinum card across the hotel desk to the young woman on the other side. Her name tag reads *MALLORY* in all caps, and she types furiously, searching for something on her computer.

"I know. I'm sorry, Mrs. Augustus, but the hotel is unfortunately sold out tonight. There's a concert up the street, and we don't have any more junior suites available. That would be the next level up from what you booked."

Ophelia Augustus lets out a low growl as she pushes her short silver hair behind her ears. She can't believe how incompetent this hotel is. The St. Simon is supposed to be one of the most luxurious and regal hotels in Texas, but they can't even keep their obligations to their most exclusive customers. How ridiculous.

Ophelia leans across the hotel desk and whispers to Mallory, her voice low. "I don't want to be this person, but do you know who I am?" she asks, cocking her head to the side.

Mallory shrugs. "No, ma'am, I'm sorry, but I don't."

Ophelia lets out a deep sigh. "My husband is Austin Augustus. You know, the Austin Augustus."

A blank look falls over Mallory's face.

"He was the Governor of Georgia for three terms," Ophelia says.

"Oh, sure. Yes. I remember him," Mallory replies, her brow furrowed.

A liar. Ophelia can sniff them out easily.

"Yes, he's going to join me after his board meeting ends sometime tomorrow evening, and he will be so upset if the room isn't upgraded. He'll be furious, *and you know he talks to a lot of people*, and I would just hate to have him speak poorly about what appears to be such a lovely establishment," Ophelia says as she gestures around the grand foyer.

"I see," Mallory says with a tight smile. "Let me see what I can do." She returns to typing furiously as Ophelia lets her eyes wander around the lobby. She had read about the St. Simon in *Condé Nast Traveler*, and it had always been on her bucket list. She couldn't bear to have just an ordinary room in one of Texas's most historic hotels. *The trip would effectively be useless.*

Sure, she was here to see her daughter, Liberty, as he graduated from Lonestar State College, but it was also about the experience.

And if the lobby of the St. Simon was anything like the rooms, Ophelia knew she was in for a treat. The lobby unfolded beneath crystal chandeliers that cast glimmers of light across marble floors polished to a pristine shine. Antebellum-inspired furnishings such as plush velvet settees and hand-carved mahogany tables invited guests to linger, while attentive staff in crisp white uniforms moved with practiced grace. The air carried hints of magnolia blossoms and aged bourbon. Guests spoke in hushed tones, *as if the hotel demanded reverence*. Their voices mingled with the gentle notes from a baby grand piano played by a white-gloved musician in the corner.

"Mrs. Augustus," Mallory says with a bright smile. "I have great news."

Ophelia turns her attention back to the hotel desk. "Yes! I knew you could do it!" she says, smiling wide. *The name drop always works*, even if the silly young clerk behind the desk has no recollection of the distinguished Augustus family from Decatur, Georgia.

"We are going to put you in our most luxurious room: the Presidential Suite."

Ophelia's heart flutters. Every time she drops her husband's name, service workers move mountains to ensure they can accommodate each and every request.

"That is fabulous," Ophelia says.

"This room typically goes for around eight to ten thousand dollars per night," Mallory says as she hands Ophelia a hotel key card across the desk.

"Amazing! Now, Mallory, do you think you could send me up a bottle of champagne too?"

"There's already one in the room, ma'am."

CHAPTER 2

O phelia left the lobby with a skip in her step. The Presidential Suite! Oh, how Austin would love this. Maybe even their daughter, Liberty, could come stay with them for a bit after her graduation. The last time Ophelia stayed in a presidential suite, it had three rooms, a kitchen, and a balcony that overlooked Rue Montorgueil when she went to Paris for *a girls' trip* with her younger sister, Lynn. They had a lovely time at La Maison Étoilée, *another hotel in the Astor network.*

Ophelia walks toward the elevators at the end of the hall, her purse in one hand and her hotel keys in the other. MALLORY had instructed the bellhop to bring her bags up to the Presidential Suite so Ophelia wouldn't have to lift a finger. How lovely.

Just as she reaches the end of the hallway where the two gold-trimmed elevators sit, something catches her eye, and her ear. It's a dark mahogany bar that looks a little like a speakeasy. Inside, an older Black gentleman sits in the corner playing the cello, while a few patrons linger at the bar and on the plush leather couches that line the walls of the cozy haunt.

The sweet sound of the cello tugs at her heart. It reminds her of her time at Bryn Mawr in the seventies, when she was a member of the classical music program.

She pauses in the hall.

A scotch sounds so lovely right now. Especially with a bit of live cello in the background.

Ophelia decides to stroll into the cozy little speakeasy. Her leather loafers scuff against the hardwood floor as she walks up to the bar and pulls herself onto one of the tall barstools. At only five foot five, she lets her legs dangle above the ground as she waits for the young Black woman behind the bar to finish serving another customer.

As Ophelia looks around, she notices a few odd trinkets lining the back of the bar. A wine glass in the shape of a skull. A little jack-o'-lantern light sits next to rows of liquor. It's May. Nowhere near the Halloween season.

The bartender finishes up with another customer and begins walking toward Ophelia. The woman behind the bar is quite stunning, with long braids pulled back into a ponytail at the top of her head and bright brown eyes that seem to glow in the low light of the bar. She lets out a bright white grin as she approaches and pulls out a menu.

"Hi there," the bartender says. "I'm Savannah. How can I help you tonight?" She slides the menu across the mahogany wood bar to Ophelia, who picks it up with curiosity.

The menu is a thick black leather book with **THE PHANTOM** embossed in bright silver on the cover.

"The Phantom!" Ophelia laughs as she picks up the tome. She reaches into her coat pocket, pulls out her reading glasses, and sets them on the bridge of her nose. "What a curious name for a hotel bar!"

Savannah nods and rests her hands on the edge of the bar. "Well, you know the stories about the St. Simon, don't you?"

Ophelia frowns. "Stories?"

"Well," Savannah says as she pours a glass of water from a large pitcher on the bar, "we have three types of clients at the St. Simon. Affluent people who read about us in *Condé Nast*, businessmen, and ghost hunters."

Ophelia blinks, unable to process what Savannah has just told her. *"Ghost hunters?"*

Savannah smiles. "Hence the name of the bar you're sitting in. The Phantom." She opens the menu to a page with a list of cocktails. "Each of our cocktails is named after different ghosts that haunt the hotel. The Lady in Pink is my favorite."

Ophelia frowns. If she hadn't been granted the Presidential Suite, she would have left in an instant. A haunted hotel? How ridiculous. Advertisements for the St. Simon should clearly mention that it is haunted. It's a liability, isn't it? Allowing people to stay in a hotel that is *infested*?

"I'm not really interested in this type of stuff," Ophelia says as she folds the menu closed and slides it back to the bartender. "I'd just like a scotch on the rocks, please."

"No worries," Savannah says with a tight grin. "No one has really ever had a problem since I've been here."

"Well. I'd sure hope not."

"All of the rooms where they've seen ghosts, they don't rent them out anymore unless they're really, really in a bind."

Savannah turns and pours a glass of scotch over ice, then slides it across the bar to Ophelia, who picks it up slowly with a concerned look.

"Well… *how haunted* are we talking here?" Ophelia asks.

Savannah lets out a little laugh. "I mean, mostly friendly ghosts. Have you seen *Casper?*"

Ophelia frowns. "Cartoons aren't really my thing." She takes a long sip of her scotch. "Is this Glenfiddich?"

Savannah nods.

Ophelia's face twists like she just ate a sour candy. "It tastes like Crown Royal. Ugh."

"Do you want something else?" Savannah asks.

Ophelia shakes her head. "No. I've accepted that this is just not going to be a pleasant stay for me. Bad scotch. Ghosts. What next?"

Savannah shrugs. "Well, I think we have mostly Caspers at the St. Simon. What room are you staying in?" she asks, tilting her head to the side.

"The Presidential Suite."

Savannah frowns and looks down at the keycard sitting on the bar, as if her eyes can't believe what they're seeing. "Room 777?"

Ophelia shrugs and glances at the keycard. She flips over the cardstock key holder to reveal 777 scribbled on the back. She holds the card up to show Savannah.

Savannah slowly shakes her head, her braids swaying behind her. "You can't stay there," she whispers. "You can't stay in that room."

Ophelia's eyes widen, and she leans across the bar, her worn and wrinkled hands gripping the bar top. "What do you mean?"

"What I mean is that room is haunted. The most haunted hotel room in Texas. We have professional ghost hunters who *refuse to stay* there. They aren't even supposed to be renting it out."

CHAPTER 3

───────◆───────

"I need a different room," Ophelia says as she leans over the hotel desk, staring eye-to-eye with a large Russian man who has replaced MALLORY. Her head swirls from the scotch she downed just moments ago. She feels her face grow hot, itchy, and irritated. Her hands feel dry and scaly. She shifts in her leather loafers as her heart races.

What a complete mess of a night. She should be sitting in the bar, listening to the sweet sounds of the cello while she finishes her drink; not begging some overgrown man in a suit to give her a new room.

This is supposed to be the pinnacle of luxury, not some sort of teenage prank. How could they put her in a room that's *haunted*?

"What is wrong with the room?" the man asks in a thick Eastern European accent. "It's a lovely room. No one ever complains about the Presidential Suite."

"Well… I've been told that the room is *haunted*," Ophelia says. She slides the cardstock key holder over to the man and crosses her arms across her chest. "I will not be staying anywhere that's cursed. That's ridiculous. You shouldn't be renting that room out, and you definitely shouldn't be allowing your staff to tell people they're staying in a House of Horrors. I want a refund, a new room, and to speak with the manager."

The man nods. Ophelia catches a glimpse of his name tag: IVAN. She leans across the desk as she watches him tap around on his computer.

"I am the manager," he says, letting out a small smile.

"I see," Ophelia grumbles. "I know earlier I said I needed an upgrade, but I will just take my original room that I had reserved. That will be just fine."

Ivan frowns and shakes his head. "I'm sorry, ma'am, that room is no longer available."

Ophelia sighs. "Really? I've only been gone for forty minutes! I—"

"There's a concert in town, and rooms are sold out all across the city."

"Well, surely someone will have something available. I'll go to another hotel. Just refund my card and I—"

"Isn't your husband meeting you here? Governor… Augustus, is it?" Ivan raises his eyebrows.

Does he know?

Ophelia's stomach turns. "Yes, I suppose."

"Well, you don't want to switch hotels when he might already be on his way here, Mrs. Augustus. I can assure you that the Presidential Suite will meet his utmost expectations. Plus, every hotel in the city is just about sold out. Everything except for *The Alamo Motel*."

"Ugh," Ophelia grumbles.

The Alamo Motel. She'd driven by the wretched dump on accident. She took a wrong turn through a bad neighborhood, and there it was, standing in all its degenerate glory. A rundown A-frame hellhole with stained siding and *lingerers* sitting in white plastic chairs outside the rooms.

Ophelia shudders at the thought.

Bed bugs.

Rats.

Roaches.

Black mold.

Prostitutes.

"I would never stay there," Ophelia says. "The thought of it! Just horrible. Even when I was a broke college student at Bryn Mawr, I would never stay at a place like that. I'd rather stay in a whorehouse. You really have nothing else available?"

Ivan shakes his head. "I promise, Ms. Augustus. You're going to love it. Just give it a chance."

CHAPTER 4

O phelia had no desire to stay in any room of the St. Simon
Hotel, never mind the Presidential Suite. You wouldn't
stay at a hotel infested with bed bugs, would you? You wouldn't
stay at a bed and breakfast that just so happened to be flooded
with cockroaches, would you? Then why on Earth would
someone pay money to stay at a hotel infested with ghosts?

As Ophelia walks down the long hallway on the top floor
of the hotel, she ponders just that. How is this hotel even at
capacity? Are that many people really trying to sleep with ghosts
in their room? Maybe they don't know. If that's the case, maybe
it's a class action lawsuit waiting to happen. Ophelia decides it's
something she'll have to *ask Austin when he arrives*.

She grumbles as her leather loafers scuff along the
patterned carpet that lines the long corridor. It feels seemingly
endless, almost bending over the horizon. She hates big hotels
for this. Everything is monotonous. Everything is the same.

Ophelia didn't choose the St. Simon for monotony. She chose it for luxury. *She wanted an experience.*

When she arrives at the end of the hall, at room 777, her stomach turns. She looks down at the cardstock key holder in her freckled, pasty hands. Is she really going to do this?

Ophelia peers over her shoulder, checking to make sure nothing is following her. When she realizes she appears to be alone, she slides the key card into the door, pushes down the gold handle, and crosses the threshold into the Presidential Suite.

Her eyes widen.

It's more beautiful than she could have imagined. A crystal chandelier hangs in the middle of the foyer, welcoming her into the vast, open space. From just inside the entryway, she can already see that the "room" is not really a room at all. Heck, a suite doesn't even sound right.

This is 3,000 square feet of pure luxury. The frown fades from her face.

In the middle of the foyer, there's a round wooden table with a bouquet of big, beautiful magnolias. Next to the flowers is a generous cornucopia of local artisan goods; Mexican chocolate, crackers, cheese, and even a small jar of caviar. And then, a big, beautiful bottle of wine: a Bordeaux from Richard Astor's own vineyard in Napa.

Big and beautiful. That's everything in this stunning suite.

Ophelia's heart flutters. She can't wait to try it. How did they know she loved Bordeaux? She picks up the bottle and gazes at it, a fond memory stirring in her heart. France. With Austin, about twenty years ago. When he was Governor, the French government offered him a trip to meet with some politicians about something or other, Ophelia can't quite recall what, but she does remember the wine. She remembers begging Austin to take her with him.

When he was Governor, he was so busy. So distant. So detached.

But he surprised her.

After he finished his official business in Paris, they took a trip to the French wine country and stayed for a week, drinking and sampling all the lovely wines across the region.

She misses it.

She misses him.

A small tear wells in her eye, and she shakes it off. The scotch. It's made her emotional.

Next to the basket is a small letter.

Ophelia takes her glasses out of her jacket pocket and sets them on the bridge of her nose. She picks up the letter, which reads:

"Dear Mr. Clark,"

Ophelia looks up from the letter and frowns. Mr. Clark? She shakes her head and continues.

> "We hope you enjoy your stay in the most beautiful room on our property. The Presidential Suite is one of the most exquisite hotel rooms south of the Mason-Dixon Line. We have done our best to ensure that every detail of the room is up to the highest standard. If anything does not meet your expectations, I ask that you reach out to me personally and I will ensure that you have the best experience possible. Thank you for staying with us at the St. Simon.
>
> Sincerely,
> Myra — Manager of the St. Simon

Ophelia frowned and put the letter back on the table. *Mr. Clark? Myra? Was this an old letter? Or was Ivan lying to her about being the manager? More incompetence from what should be a four-star hotel.*

But as mad and irritated as Ophelia wants to be, she can't help but look around the room and bask in the luxury. Sure, the hotel isn't the best with details, and maybe it might be *haunted*… but what could Ophelia do about it?

Not much.

CHAPTER 5

O phelia sits on the edge of the bed in the master bedroom as she sips her glass of wine. It's not bad for hotel wine, though it's a bit bitter for her liking. Everything Astor is supposed to represent the pinnacle of luxury, and yet the wine falls a bit flat.

At the end of every sip, there's a pungent punch that lingers on her tongue with just a hint of vinegar. Is the wine bad? Every few minutes, she looks down at the glass and wonders if she's sipping rancid wine, or if it's her own subconscious hoping the hotel would mess up just one more time, giving her an excuse to leave an even worse review than she was already planning.

As she sits, sipping her wine, she begins to draft a review for the hotel on her small Android phone. Two and a half stars. Maybe three. But probably two and a half.

Ophelia Augustus is one of the top-ranked reviewers on *Hotel Finder,* with thousands of loyal followers. She never considered herself tech-savvy, but when a few of her witty and snarky reviews gained attention, she attracted a respectable following on the platform.

"While the St. Simon did provide a complimentary bottle of wine, it was pleasant at first but finished with a slightly rancid aftertaste."

"The hotel staff was underwhelming. One employee even informed me that my room was haunted, which caused me significant emotional distress."

"This so-called 'haunted hotel' is not labeled as such anywhere on their website, leading me to wonder: what exactly are they trying to hide?"

Ophelia takes a long sip of her second glass of wine, or is it her third? She can't remember.

She looks out into the vast suite, taking in the room. The master bedroom sits next to a grand study that opens into the living room. In the library are all the classics you could dream of, shelved in thick leatherbound books with exquisite gold embossing. *Little Women, Wuthering Heights, A Tree Grows in Brooklyn* — it's as if the staff at the St. Simon had hand-selected Ophelia's favorites and made sure they were perfectly displayed on the tall mahogany bookshelves.

"Despite these challenges, the Presidential Suite was exquisitely designed in a way that felt almost… personal…"

Just as she is about to draft a snarky line about how the hotel had addressed their welcome note to the wrong guest, she notices it.

It's about the size of a thumb.

A big, meaty thumb.

The kind you'd find on a heavyset, overweight man with a bulging beer belly.

It's brown and black, with a thick hardshell armor, and it's crawling across the floor with two little antennae careening over its head, gently dusting the marble as it walks.

A roach.

In her room.

In the Presidential Suite.

Ophelia jumps up from the bed, spilling the glass of red wine across the white comforter like bloodstains. She kicks off one of her leather loafers and runs toward the roach. Gripping the thick sole, she slams it down on the insect again and again until the little bug is pulverized like ground meat, its innards splattered across the pristine marble floor.

CHAPTER 6

O phelia grips the phone so tightly her knuckles turn white. "I am in the Presidential Suite, room 777, and there was a cock-a-roach in my room. I demand a new room immediately. There is an infestation!"

"Ms. Augustus…"

"MRS. Augustus," Ophelia growls.

Ivan takes a deep breath on the other end of the line. "I can assure you, ma'am, that there are no cockroaches at the St. Simon or in the Presidential Suite. Our hotel routinely undergoes inspections for these sorts of things, and I can guarantee you that there are no cockroaches in your room."

Ophelia frowns and takes a deep, hearty breath. "I am looking right at one!" she yells.

She grips the phone and turns back around, walking to the edge of the bed, the scene of the crime. The spot where she had pulverized the little vermin intruder into a pulp.

Except when she returns to inspect the body... it's not there. The roach has disappeared. The guts that had splattered across the cold ivory tiles are gone.

"Mrs. Augustus, are you there?" Ivan says.

Ophelia narrows her eyes. Is she drunk? Hallucinating? Delusional? Her mother died of Alzheimer's. Is she suffering a similar fate? The thought makes her heart drop.

"Yes. I'm here. I demand to be compensated for the roach in my room. I am staying at a luxury resort, not the goddamn Alamo Motel."

"I understand, Mrs. Augustus—"

Before Ivan can finish speaking, the doorbell rings. It's so loud it makes Ophelia jump.

"I've sent up a bottle of Glenfiddich 21 for the inconvenience."

Glenfiddich.

Ophelia smiles from ear to ear. She didn't really get to enjoy her scotch earlier, with the interruption and all. Maybe she can put on a little nice music on the television, there's even a record player in the living room. They've got a bunch of classics. It sounds lovely.

"Well, thank you, Ivan. I'm still a bit shaken up, but a nice glass of scotch will certainly help."

CHAPTER 7

In a peculiar way, Ophelia Augustus feels a pull in her heart to keep drinking. Is she bored? Lonely? Scared? Maybe all of the above. But before she realizes what she's doing, Ophelia finishes the entire bottle of Bordeaux and starts working on her second glass of Glenfiddich.

She changes into one of the lovely cloth robes she finds in the bathroom and settles into the plush California king like the queen she believes herself to be. Sipping the peaty scotch, she flips through the channels on the television, looking for nothing in particular. In fact, she's so slurred, so slow, so inebriated, she doesn't even realize what she's watching—or when she's flipping through the channels at all.

With a deep breath and a shaky hand, Ophelia finally flicks off the light switch, leaving only the television's blue glow to push back the darkness of the master bedroom. The vastness of the suite suddenly feels oppressive rather than luxurious, its empty rooms stretching out around her like a labyrinth. For the first time in years, she feels utterly, completely alone.

For once, she feels small.

Back home in Decatur, she lives in an even bigger house — but it's different. In Decatur, she's not alone. There's Rosie, the house manager, who lives in a nice little guest house at the back of the property. There's José, the gardener, who wakes up every morning at the crack of dawn to ensure that each blade of grass on the front lawn is perfectly manicured and pristine. The former head of the HOA, Ophelia takes pride in the fact that she has the most beautiful house in the neighborhood by far.

Austin spent his career in oil and worked hard for many years to ensure they had a lovely, bright white Antebellum home that stood tall among a sea of perfectly pristine green grass, like a beacon of excellence in the neighborhood.

Despite her occasionally ornery attitude, Ophelia is grateful for Austin in every way. He provided her with the means to live the life she dreamed of as a little girl.

Her mind wanders as she takes another sip of her scotch.

She looks down at her phone.

It's almost two o'clock in the morning.

Her heart flutters. Austin. She has to call him. He must be so worried. She was supposed to call when she got to the room, but with the haunting and everything, it had slipped her mind.

She reaches for the phone on the marble nightstand next to the master bed and fumbles with it in her hands. The graphics on the screen sway and swoon as her vision blurs.

404…

404…

Her mind draws a blank. What is his goddamn phone number?

Contacts. Right. She flicks to the contacts app and scrolls to *Austin*.

Ring.

Ring.

"Oh, please pick up," she mumbles. "Please pick up. I need you."

Ring.

Ring.

Ring.

"The number you called did not answer. Please hang up and try again later."

"Bastard!" Ophelia says as she quickly hangs up the phone. She hates it when he does this. He should be waiting for her to call, checking in on her, making sure she's okay while she's staying in this big old hotel room all by herself. Isn't that what husbands are for? To be there for their wives? To call them at the end of a busy day and tell them they can't wait to see them?

Ophelia slams the phone down on the bed. She picks up the crystal cocktail glass and takes one final, long sip, finishing what's left of the amber liquor. Her head feels heavy. Dense. Like too much is floating around in her brain.

She feels her head tipping backward, the weight of it pulling her down, collapsing her into the fluffy white comforter. She surrounds herself in the luxury she so deeply desires as she drifts off into the deepest, darkest, most sinister sleep.

CHAPTER 8

S irens blare loudly. Then a banging. A loud banging.
Ophelia can't open her eyes. They're too heavy, stuck like glue to her eyeballs. Too drugged from too much Bordeaux and scotch. A sour stench wafts through her nostrils—is it mold? Mildew?

And then she feels it.

At first, it's just a tickle, like a luxurious down feather brushing her forehead.

Until there are more of them, moving in sinister unison across her skin. Tiny legs crawl across her face as an army of cockroaches marches to war.

Ophelia opens one eye, then the other. What she sees takes her breath away. She blinks. Then blinks again.

But nothing changes.

She quickly sits up in the bed as a rush of nausea hits her. Her stomach churns, and vomit bubbles in her throat. As she moves, cockroaches tumble from her forehead and into her lap, squealing and squirming.

She screams and flings them off the bed and onto the floor.

But it's not the floor of the Presidential Suite.

It's a green, shaggy carpet that looks like something out of a seventies movie. There are crumbs embedded in the fibers and even bits of dirt. Wood paneling lines the small room — maybe two or three hundred square feet at most. Ophelia sits on a small, full-sized bed with cheap, papery sheets speckled with little red stains.

Bed bugs.

Ophelia looks around the room in horror, her mouth agape. Her beautiful and exquisite luxury hotel has evaporated and transformed into a cheap, dreadful motel. Thick black curtains cover the windows, blocking out any hint of daylight. The only illumination comes from a small lamp on the nightstand beside the bed.

Under the lamp is a Bible, leatherbound with gold embossing. It looks completely out of place, like it belongs on the wall of the Presidential Suite's study, not in this horrid place.

She brings her hands to her face. She wants to scream, but her throat feels empty. Has she been kidnapped? Drugged? Was it that bastard Russian, Ivan? Something looked off about him. Sinister.

Ophelia takes a deep breath, and before she can fully assess her surroundings, the loud banging at the door resumes.

"OPHELIA AUGUSTUS. OPEN UP!" yells a man from the other side of the room's metal door.

Chills run down her spine.

Is it her kidnapper?

Was she brought here by some man?

The door is a dark blue, its paint chipped and peeling. As the man continues banging, Ophelia becomes certain that whoever wants to come in could do so with sheer force if they tried hard enough.

She slides off the bed. Her leather loafers are gone. She has to walk barefoot across the filthy carpet, crunching over crumbs and the creeping, crawling bugs breeding in the shag. She hears them pop beneath her feet, a sickening burst of guts squishing into the carpet and smearing across the soles of her feet.

Careful not to make too much noise, she tiptoes toward the door, hoping the man won't hear her approach.

"OPHELIA. OPEN THE DOOR."

When she reaches the door and looks through the tiny brass peephole, she doesn't see the hallway of the St. Simon Hotel, or anything remotely like it. Instead, she sees a porch. One of those outdoor walkways that line budget motels in the South, like a Motel 8. There's a white brass railing and a strip of fake green grass carpeting the path outside.

It's dark outside. So dark that Ophelia can't even make out a parking lot or a hotel sign. There is no moon, no stars. Is she still in Houston? She can't tell.

It's just the porch.

And the man.

He looks to be about six foot five, taller than Ivan, with thick, meaty hands, a bald head, and a Glock on his hip. He wears a battered plaid shirt, grease stains running down the front. The man balls his hand into a fist again and slams it against the peephole so hard it startles Ophelia, causing her to stumble backward.

"I SEE YOU," he yells. "Open up."

Words stick in the back of her throat like taffy, but eventually, she stutters them out. "I w-w-won't. Who are you? Why d-d-did you bring me here?"

She looks back through the peephole and sees the man's wide, toothy smile. Some of his teeth are missing. Most are stained yellow, with little bits caught between them, like he just ate a sloppy, meaty sandwich.

"I didn't bring you here," he growls. "You came here all on your own."

His words hit her in the gut. On her own? Did she leave the Presidential Suite? Her head pounds. She can't remember. All she recalls is the scotch and the Bordeaux and how easily she had guzzled it down. Bile bubbles in her stomach as she tries to piece together what happened the night before. Or is it the same night? It's so dark outside, she can't tell.

"Let me go then, if you didn't bring me here," Ophelia says. "And I won't call the cops. I won't call the police. Just let me go."

The man nods, and the thick wrinkles in his bald head scrunch together as a smirk spreads across his face. He brings his fat pink lips close to the peephole and whispers:

"Two million dollars."

"What?" Ophelia says, stepping back from the door.

"Two million dollars, and I'll let you out of here."

Ophelia shakes her head, her sandy silver curls trembling with her. "I—I don't have that kind of money."

"Liar. Don't you live at 4657 Plumberry Lane?"

Ophelia swallows hard.

"Wasn't your husband the Governor of Georgia before he became a top lobbyist for big tech and oil?"

"I—uh."

"Wire me the money, and I will let you out. Or else I will make my way in.

CHAPTER 9

---•---

Before Austin Augustus served as the Governor of Georgia, he had a brief stint in President George Bush's administration as the Ambassador to Great Britain. Ophelia was delighted about the appointment, she loved London, and she loved the idea of being an ambassador's wife.

When the Twin Towers were struck on September 11th, Augustus was in Washington on official duties. He called her late that afternoon to give her an update on what was happening.

It was one of the most terrifying times in Ophelia's life. Sitting there in Decatur, wondering what her husband was doing in Washington. Would planes strike the building he was in, just like they struck the Pentagon and the World Trade Center? Her mind reeled as she sat at home, worrying and waiting. This was before cellphones became popular. She couldn't text him. Her only option was to call when he was free and out of meetings. She had never been so scared in her life.

Except now.

Sitting on the edge of a dingy motel mattress. Who knows how many hookers have slept in this bed? The deeds that must have been done here make Ophelia's skin crawl.

But one thing sticks in her mind as she sits hopelessly on the edge of the bed: Austin's words. His long southern drawl, repeated often whenever he helped her make sense of foreign policy and what was happening in global politics during his time in Washington.

"Never negotiate with terrorists."

Austin would say it all the time. In fact, even after he left politics, it became a phrase he used often. In business negotiations. Even in parenting.

One time, when their eldest son, Jeremy, locked himself in his room because they wouldn't let him take the car out after midnight, he screamed and yelled and whined like the spoiled son he was. Austin just left him crying. No matter how loud. It was so loud, in fact, that one of the neighbors even called the police.

But Austin didn't care.

"Never negotiate with terrorists," he said in his long southern drawl. "Eventually that boy will get so damn tired of whining and moaning he'll shut himself up."

As Ophelia sits on the crunchy, stained motel comforter, she reminds herself of this while rubbing her wrinkled hands.

She will not negotiate with terrorists.

And the man outside is a fucking terrorist.

Maybe I'm a political prisoner.

Maybe it's an evil oil baron's thug who brought me here.

Her mind drifts, floating through the twisty plots of the thriller novels she used to read on Myrtle Beach holidays. She looks around the wretched motel room for an escape plan. She has to get out. The smell alone is making her woozy, like mold and dirty feet.

There is a phone on the nightstand.

She wants to pick it up and call 911. But surely the man outside would hear her. Would he beat down the door? Bust through the windows?

Small and frail, Ophelia stands no chance against the bulky, bearded man.

But it's worth a shot, isn't it?

Maybe if she screams loud enough, someone else in the motel will hear and come to her rescue.

Then again, who stays in motels like this? People running from the law, she thinks. With her luck, yelling for help will only summon more criminals to this wretched hellhole.

But she has to try, doesn't she?

She could try the phone. And if that doesn't work, then maybe the money. She doesn't want to negotiate with her captor, it feels wrong, but if she gets out of here, she can find a way to recover the money. Call the police. Seek justice. She can do it, if she tries.

The phone on the nightstand seems to grow larger, looming toward her. Beckoning her to pick it up and call for help.

With care, Ophelia rises to her feet and tiptoes toward the phone. Who could she call? 911? Austin? Her daughter?

Heck—she might be in Mexico for all she knows. There's no telling how long she's been unconscious.

Or… she could call the front desk.

Ophelia grabs the bright red phone. It feels like it's pulsing in her hand. On the base is a button labeled *FRONT DESK*. Her heart pounds against her ribs, and she presses the button, unsure of what to expect.

The phone rings.

And rings.

And rings.

And then—a voice on the other end.

"Hello, Mrs. Augustus. Are you ready for your meal?" says a soft female voice.

"My what?" Ophelia whispers, her voice cracking.

"Your meal. It's just about ready. I was going to send it up for you. Our chef has been working all night to make you the most delicious—"

"I don't need that," Ophelia says, her voice trembling. "I don't need that. I need you to call the police and send someone here now. There's a very large man who has trapped me in my room. I need to get out. He's threatening me. He says he wants my money. I need to get out of here—"

"I'm sorry, ma'am. While that does sound awful, that's not something I can help with. But your food will be there shortly."

CHAPTER 9

When Ophelia puts down the phone, a tear falls down her cheek. Where is she? And how could this place be so damn cruel?

A rustling comes from outside the door.

Quickly, Ophelia sits on the dingy bed and places her hands in her lap. That's when she notices something peculiar. The solid, blue, paint-chipped door has changed. Not much, but just enough for her to notice.

At the bottom of the door is a metal slot, like the kind used to slide a tray of food to a prisoner in a cell.

A *prison.*

It dawns on her like a brick to the head.

She is in a prison.

The rustling outside pushes open the small metal flap, and a tray appears.

Ophelia's stomach turns. She is a bit hungry. After all, she hadn't eaten much, and the liquor still stains her stomach like oily bile.

But when she peers over the bed to see what her captors have delivered, her stomach sinks. On the metal tray isn't much of a meal at all. Just a plastic plate, covered in cardboard dust.

Two loud bangs rattle the door.

"EAT UP, BUTTERCUP!" the man yells from outside.

He laughs, and his voice fades as if he's walking away from the door.

Ophelia looks down at the plate of cardboard shavings.

Now what?

Using her foot, she carefully moves the cardboard off the plate, hoping to reveal a clue or message. But beneath the mess is only a plain white plate.

She listens as the footsteps fade.

She rushes to the door and looks through the peephole.

The man is gone.

Quickly, she grips the door handle, praying it will turn and release her from this nightmare.

It won't.

The handle is jammed. She is locked in, from the inside.

Her heart plummets.

Is this how she will die?

In this hellhole?

She can't bear the thought.

And Liberty. Oh, Liberty. It hits her in the gut. Did she miss her daughter's graduation? Surely Liberty would call someone if she didn't show up. Surely there would be some sort of search.

Liberty's graduation, she wouldn't miss it for the world. Growing up, Liberty always struggled in school. Not because she lacked intelligence, quite the opposite, but because her dyslexia and social anxiety created constant obstacles. There were times when Austin and Ophelia doubted she would even finish high school.

To miss Liberty's graduation now would make Ophelia feel like the worst mother on Earth.

She wants to collapse on the bed. To cry. To will herself out of this hell. She wants to negotiate with the terrorists.

But then an idea flashes through her mind.

The window.

She can climb out the window.

Ophelia walks to the right of the door and pulls back the blue curtains, revealing the night's dense darkness. She opens the window, letting a gust of cool air whip into the room with a harsh, bitter blow.

Just as she's about to throw her leg over the windowsill and embrace her freedom, she notices something strange. There's no porch. In fact, there's no anything. No parking lot. No railing. No motel. Just complete and total darkness. A void.

If she steps through the window, she will be stepping into the unknown. Into nothing.

Ophelia stumbles back, her head swooning. Something isn't right. Her body feels wrong. Her skin itches and pulls tight across her bones. Something is happening inside her that she can't explain. A rumbling in her stomach. A pounding in her head. Her skin crawls, as though a thousand centipedes are lodged beneath the surface.

It's not the liquor.

No. This is something else.

Her vision blurs. The room stretches and warps, bending like a funhouse mirror. A buzzing fills her ears. She tries to call out, but her throat clamps shut.

She stumbles back from the window. Her wedding ring, the three-carat diamond Austin gave her on their twentieth anniversary, slips off her finger. It doesn't just fall; it crashes to the carpet with a sound like a bowling ball.

Ophelia stares down at her hands.

They're shrinking.

She's shrinking.

The dingy motel bed becomes a vast continent of stained fabric. The ceiling pulls away as if it's being yanked into the sky. Her clothes don't shrink with her. They hang from her body and then drop away completely as she dwindles down to the size of a field mouse, maybe smaller.

The carpet beneath her bare feet is now a jungle of coarse fibers. A roach lumbers past, big as a Cadillac, its feelers twitching and pulsing with fury.

Ophelia tries to scream, but all that escapes is a high-pitched squeak that no one will ever hear

CHAPTER 10

As if things weren't already horrible, Ophelia is now nothing more than the size of a bug in the vast, wretched room. Cockroaches crawl past her on the floor like busy workers on their way to the office. The window now sits so far above her that it's completely out of reach, her one escape. Into what? Nothingness? Oblivion?

Ophelia holds herself tightly and closes her eyes.

This has to be a dream.

Close your eyes.

And then open them.

It will all be over.

But when Ophelia opens her eyes, she's still standing in the motel room. The strands of the shaggy carpet rise like long grass, and walking through them with her little spiny legs feels like trudging through molasses.

The doorknob rattles, pulling her attention from the nightmare around her. Someone is trying to get in.

A knock at the door.

It's so loud that it shakes the room, and tiny Ophelia feels every vibration ripple through her minuscule body.

"HOUSEKEEPING!" booms a voice from outside.

Ophelia's stomach turns, but a flicker of hope rises in her chest. Maybe the maid can help her. Maybe someone will rescue her.

"Come in," Ophelia says. Her small voice clicks faintly through the air, barely audible, only a few roaches hiding under the bed even seem to notice.

Suddenly, the door bursts open and a woman appears in the doorway. She looks to be in her sixties, maybe a bit younger than Ophelia. She wears a maroon polo shirt with a small logo stitched over the right breast. Ophelia can't make out the word without her glasses.

In the woman's right hand is a clunky metal vacuum with a large cloth bag. The kind you'd find in an old vacuum store in the eighties. Ophelia remembers having one just like it, forty years ago.

Ophelia takes a step toward the maid and looks up at her, craning her neck all the way back. By Ophelia's estimate, the maid is probably five foot four, and poor Ophelia is no more than two inches tall.

"Help!" Ophelia yells with every bone in her body. It echoes through the room like a faint click.

The maid doesn't stir.

She doesn't look down.

She simply plugs the old, rickety vacuum into an outlet in the wall and switches on the roaring machine.

The sound is deafening. It makes Ophelia want to scream. It takes the breath out of her tiny body.

She watches as the bugs begin to scatter, skittering away from the loud machine barreling toward them.

Ophelia looks up at the maid one more time and waves her arms in the air frantically. "Hey! Down here! Help!"

But the maid ignores her and turns the vacuum directly toward Ophelia.

The vacuum hurtles forward like a freight train, roaring and ripping. Its gaping metal mouth hungers for anything in its path. Her tiny legs scramble beneath her, propelling her toward the room's only potential source of safety, under the bed.

The machine draws closer, and the suction tugs at her, yanking her backward toward certain death. Ophelia lets out a squeak that would've been a scream if she were her normal size.

The roaches scatter around her, darting in chaotic patterns across the carpet jungle. And for once in her goddamn life, Ophelia follows their lead.

She dives under the bed just as the vacuum's roar crescendos behind her. The rush of air ruffles her sandy and silver curls. Under the bed, dust bunnies, the size of actual bunnies, surround her, along with cigarette butts and crumbs.

The roaches huddle in the darkness, their armored bodies glistening under a thin shaft of light that cuts through the gloom. Ophelia backs herself against the wall, panting, her mind reeling.

And then she notices it.

The door.

The maid has left it wide open.

Ophelia begins to walk toward the edge of the bed, calculating the distance with her beady little eyes. What would have been a ten-second stroll for normal-sized Ophelia now looks like a bloody marathon.

The vacuum snarls as it circles the room. The maid hums some off-key tune to herself as she works. Ophelia watches the woman's fat ankles, stuffed into dirty white sneakers, and waits for her moment. Her sandy silver hair, once perfectly coiffed at that salon in Decatur, now hangs in her face like cobwebs.

If Austin could see her now. Christ. The thought makes her want to laugh and cry at the same time. He'd spent his whole career in the governor's mansion, shaking hands with oil barons while she played hostess, and now look at her. Cowering under a motel bed, naked, sharing a space with actual cockroaches.

The vacuum motor cuts out.

The maid mutters something about "not getting paid enough for this shit" and moves to strip the bed.

Ophelia tenses, ready to make her move.

She may be small, but she's still an Augustus, dammit.

And Augustuses don't die in fleabag motels under beds that have seen God-knows-what over the years. With her chin up, she readies herself to scurry like hell toward that open door and whatever lies beyond it.

Now or never.

Ophelia bolts. Her tiny legs skitter across the carpet, faster than she's ever moved in her adult life. The floor feels endless, each fiber of the shag like trudging through wet sand. Her old bones groan with every powerful step.

She darts left to avoid the maid's sneaker, which comes down with a thud that shakes her entire body. Then she leaps right to dodge the impending doom of the vacuum's mouth.

The light from the hallway grows brighter. Twenty more steps. Her lungs burn. Behind her, the vacuum roars back to life. The suction tugs at her, nearly pulling her backward.

Ten more steps.

A cockroach darts past, overtaking her with ease. The little bastard. Ophelia narrows her eyes and pushes harder.

Five steps.

The maid turns, vacuum hose in hand.

Three.

Ophelia launches herself forward in a desperate dive, sailing over the metal threshold of the doorway just as the vacuum's roar crescendos behind her.

For a moment, she lies there on her back, gasping.

She brushes herself off, or tries to. What's left to brush off when you're basically naked and the size of a pecan?

The world blurs around her, and as she looks up, she realizes she isn't on the porch of the raggedy old motel.

She's somewhere else entirely.

The dingy motel room, the industrial vacuum, the surly maid, all gone.

Instead, she finds herself standing on cool marble floors beneath a crystal chandelier. The smell of scotch and fresh flowers lingers in the air. A bottle of Glenfiddich stands half-empty on an ornate coffee table high above her.

The Presidential Suite.

She's back.

CHAPTER 11

B efore Ophelia has any time to adjust to her new environment, she notices something peculiar sitting on the grand king bed in the master bedroom.

A woman? Maybe. Or is it a creature?

The woman-shaped being wears a bright white St. Simon robe. Her back is turned to Ophelia, and she's leaned over the side of the bed, munching on something loudly. Slobbering, really.

Two long antennae poke out from her sandy grey hair, each as long as a fishing rod. The creature's shoulders move in an unnatural rhythm as she feeds, the shoulder blades shifting beneath the robe. Where the fabric parts at the neck, Ophelia can see patches of hardened brown shell instead of skin, gleaming under the chandelier light.

Ophelia's stomach turns. She begins to back up toward the wall, walking slowly, scanning the room for somewhere to hide.

A voice interrupts her thoughts.

"Ophelia!" yells a man from the other room.

Suddenly, a tall, olive-skinned man enters from the adjoining space. He wears no shirt, just a towel wrapped around his waist in a loose knot. He looks much younger than Ophelia, maybe in his late forties or early fifties. His hair is slicked back, wet from the shower, water droplets still clinging to his chest.

And then, the creature on the bed turns.

She reveals two large, beady black eyes and a face that looks like a funhouse mirror version of Ophelia's own. The same thin lips. The same high cheekbones. But her mouth opens sideways instead of up and down. Mandibles click where her jaw should be, coated in something that looks sickeningly like egg yolk.

The creature cocks her head at an impossible angle, antennae swiveling toward Ophelia like satellite dishes zeroing in on a signal.

"There you are, beautiful," the man says, not to Ophelia, but to the thing on the bed. "I was wondering where you'd gone."

Ophelia's, *the real Ophelia's*, breath leaves her body.

Who is this man? What is this creature? Where is Austin?

"I'm so happy I found you at the bar. You know, I always find my best and most beautiful clients at the St. Simon," the man says as he takes a seat on the plush bed beside the creature.

He closes the gap between them and kisses her on the cheek. The antennae writhe with pleasure.

He pulls away and gazes at the beast. "Imagine, someone as beautiful as you enjoying this lovely suite all by yourself. I can't have it. Have you ever done something like this before?" he asks, his voice lowering to a whisper.

The creature smiles a toothy grin, shakes her head, and reveals rows of jagged teeth and twitching tendrils inside her mouth. She returns to furiously gnawing on the room service as if she hasn't eaten in days.

Ophelia's thoughts begin to swirl. *Is the man a prostitute? He can't be.*

She can't stop watching, can't look away. *Whatever this is, a dream, a nightmare,* she pinches her soft, wrinkled skin, hoping to wake up in her own bed. But it's no use.

She's still here.

In the Presidential Suite.

Trapped.

Her heart races.

What if Austin walks in?

And sees this abomination?

What if he thinks it's her?

What if he sees her cheating on him with this whore?

Surely, he will have a fit.

"This can't be real," Ophelia whispers. "Please, God. Please let this not be real. I'll do anything. Anything to get out of this hell."

Her eyes grow moist. Then a stream of tears begins to fall down her cheeks like a waterfall.

"God, whatever I did to deserve this… please. Please…"

She wraps her arms around her naked body, holding herself tightly.

Praying for any sign of hope.

CHAPTER 12

The loud ring of a phone interrupts Ophelia's spiral of doom. It's so loud it echoes throughout the vast suite, causing both the prostitute and the creature to jump.

The creature wrestles with the pockets of her white robe, and with her long, bug-like fingers, pulls out a phone.

Ophelia's phone.

The creature fumbles with it, then sets it on the bed. With a flick of a clawed finger, she activates speaker mode, letting the caller's voice echo throughout the Presidential Suite.

The creature can't say much, maybe a grunt or two. She doesn't speak. She only stares down at the buzzing, glowing phone, her antennae hovering over her face, bobbing and swaying with a menacing grace.

"Who is it?" the man asks, leaning toward the phone.

A voice cuts through the air.

"Mom? Mom, are you there?"

Liberty.

Ophelia's heart sinks. She starts moving toward the bed, careful to avoid drawing the attention of the man or the creature. She has to find a way onto the bed. She has to talk to Liberty, her daughter must rescue her from this nightmare.

"Mom, are you there? It's Libby. Where are you?"

Ophelia quickens her pace, running toward the bed skirt with every ounce of fire and fury left in her old body. She grabs the white cotton fabric and tries to pull herself up. It reminds her of gym class back in high school. If she can just climb the rope, the bed skirt, she can reach the mattress. She can reach her daughter.

"Sorry," the man says. "Your mother can't come to the phone right now. She's... indisposed."

"Who are you?" Liberty's voice fills the room, trembling. Ophelia can hear the tears building in her daughter's throat. "Where's my mom? She was supposed to be at my graduation, and she missed it! Put her on the phone!"

Liberty's words cut through Ophelia's heart like a knife. The sting is unbearable. Her breath catches in her chest, and with it, her grip slips from the bed skirt. Her tiny, frail body crashes to the ground with a thud.

Her hip smashes against the marble floor.

She thinks she hears a crack.

She missed it.

Liberty's graduation.

Of all her children, Ophelia never thought Liberty would be the one to graduate from college. The youngest and the most fragile, Liberty never excelled in school. In fact, she struggled. At one point, Ophelia and Austin even considered pulling her out of high school to homeschool her and help her get a GED.

But suddenly, toward the end of her senior year, something changed. A newborn fire appeared in her. A determination Ophelia had never seen before lit Liberty from within. More than anything, she wanted to succeed. To show her parents that she could thrive on her own.

Ophelia was so proud of her beautiful, smart daughter, finally stepping into her own.

As she lies on the marble floor, her hip throbbing, the cool tile sapping the warmth from her tiny body, a crushing wave of guilt settles over her.

She failed her.

She failed Liberty.

"I demand to know who you are and what you've done with my mother," Liberty's voice says, trembling. "I can't lose her. She's not well."

Not well?

The words sting.

Of course Ophelia Augustus is not well. She's the size of a bug, lying naked on the floor of a demonic hotel suite with what may be a broken hip.

"Well," the man says, "don't worry, Libby. I'm taking care of her now."

Ophelia wants to scream. She wants to run out of this hotel and straight to Liberty, wherever she is. She wants to hug her and tell her it will all be okay. That she'll never miss anything important in her life again.

"She would never be with another man," Liberty says. "She loves my father."

The man nods and pats the creature on the back, rubbing his hand in wide, massaging strokes across its scaly skin.

"Well, your mother misses your father very much," he says. "She needs comfort. It sounds like sometimes, she can't even remember that he's gone."

Silence fills the room, thick and unbearable.

Liberty says nothing.

Gone? What does that even mean?

Ophelia stares up at the ornate ceiling tiles of the Presidential Suite.

Gone?

"Yeah," Liberty says softly. "Since he died, she's just never been the same. She's been irritable. Mean, even. Like darkness has fallen over her."

The man nods.

"Can she hear me?" Liberty asks, her voice even softer now.

"No, Libby. She can't hear you," the man says, eyeing the creature, who has now turned back to obliviously munching on a bag of chips.

"I didn't even want her to come to my graduation," Liberty says. "She just complains about everything. She's so negative. And she never listens to me. You know? *Really* hears me."

Ophelia feels her throat closing. Like someone is strangling her. Holding her down against her will. Pressing her throat harder and harder onto the cold tile.

She hates her.

Her own daughter hates her.

"I wanted to introduce her to my boyfriend, but she's just too much. She's so critical. I just know she'd pick apart every little thing about me right in front of him, and it's just not fair. She'll say *Liberty* in that critical southern drawl. I've asked her so many goddamn times, it's *Libby*. It's embarrassing. But when my mother didn't show up, I just got angry. So angry. I told my own fucking boyfriend that he couldn't come to my graduation because I was afraid of how she'd act. Can you believe that?"

"I can imagine that must be very hard for you, Libby," the man says, sitting on the edge of the bed. "To have a mother who embarrasses you. Who makes you feel small. Especially after all the hard work you've done."

Libby's voice trembles. A small sniffle echoes through the phone.

"Well, I can promise you this, Libby, I will take care of your mother. And I will make sure she doesn't feel any pain ever again."

CHAPTER 12

When the man hangs up the phone, he stands from the bed and looks around the room. Like he's searching for something, or someone.

Ophelia lies on the cold tile floor. She has to move.

Or he will find her.

And then… who knows what will happen.

With every ounce of will left in her body, Ophelia forces herself to stand. She presses her hands against the cold tile and pushes up.

A crack.

Did her hip just fall back into place?

She's in so much pain. The kind that makes her want to collapse, to give up. Maybe she should. Maybe she should just die here and let whatever this man has planned for her happen.

What's the point anymore?

Her daughter hates her. She's an embarrassment. It's probably true that her other children feel the same.

But still, she has to make it out. She has to apologize. She has to make it right.

She is all Libby has left.

And then she remembers.

It hits her like a punch to the gut.

Austin is gone.

Dead.

He was never coming to stay with her in the Presidential Suite. He couldn't, because he's dead.

Ophelia begins to cry as she drags herself across the cold floor, using her arms to slide inch by inch toward the bed. It's like he's dying all over again.

How could she have forgotten?

Austin is gone.

And she is alone.

No one is coming to save her.

Just as Ophelia finds refuge beneath the dusty box spring, she sees the man lower his head on the other side, peering across the floor at her. His eyes seem to glow in the shadows of her hiding place.

Ophelia scrambles toward the center, desperate to put herself out of reach.

He shoots his arm into her sanctuary, his big, meaty hand grasping wildly for her, fingers stretching and clawing through the darkness where she cowers.

"Honey! There's a roach under the bed!" the man yells.

His eyes lock on Ophelia with intense fury. He wants her. And by the look in his eyes, he will get her, if she can't figure out a plan soon.

Ophelia pulls herself deeper into the center of the bed's underside and tucks her knees to her chest, trying to make herself as small as possible. She closes her eyes, praying to whoever will listen. Sure, she's a devout Protestant, but in times like this, she'll take what she can get.

Allah.

Buddha.

Jesus.

Anyone who will save her from this hell.

Then a voice echoes through the room, and the hair on the back of her neck stands up.

The man stops reaching. In fact, he pulls back his hand and stands upright beside the bed.

"Ophelia?" a voice says.

It's smooth like whiskey. Sweet like cinnamon. With just a hint of gruffness, like tobacco.

Ophelia begins to inch toward the edge of the bed that faces the door to the master bedroom of the Presidential Suite.

It can't be.

It can't be!

When she reaches the edge and peeks out, just enough for her head to poke free, she sees him.

He's standing in the doorway, wearing a tan suit with a brown tie and leather loafers. His sandy hair is swept neatly across his forehead, and he holds a briefcase in his hands. Instead of looking down at his wife, who cowers just inches from his feet, he looks at the creature sitting on top of the bed.

"Ophelia, this isn't you," Austin says, his voice low, a glimmer of disappointment in his face.

Ophelia wills herself out into the open and stands, staring up at her husband. The face she hasn't seen in years. The man she loved so much, who left her alone in this world, is standing here in this horrible place.

Are they in hell?

Together?

"Austin!" Ophelia yells up at the man.

He doesn't stir; he just keeps his gaze focused on the creature. "This isn't you, Ophelia. This nastiness. This degeneracy. This man, whoever he is, in your room right now, this isn't you."

"It's not me! It's not!" Ophelia yells. Tears stream down her face, falling down her neck and onto her breasts, which are cold and exposed. She lets out a guttural scream that no one hears.

"Come over here," Austin says, beckoning the creature toward him with his gentle but wrinkled hands.

Ophelia watches in horror as the creature puts down the bag of chips and rises from the bed, hobbling toward her husband.

"Look," Austin says, biting his lower lip. "I know I haven't been around that much. And I know things have been hard for us. I've been working a lot, and I haven't had time for you. But you have to drop this act. You have to drop this monstrous, hard-shelled person that you've become."

The creature walks around the bed until it's just steps away from Austin.

Ophelia, with every ounce of strength left in her body, runs in between them, standing with her little arms up in the air, shouting. "AUSTIN! I AM DOWN HERE. ME! THE REAL ME! I AM DOWN HERE."

Why can't he see her?

She wants to hug him. Kiss him. Hold him. Touch him. It has been too long. Years without him. Her everything. Her protector, her guide, her best friend, and her confidant. For the past several years, she's been living her life with a cloud cast over her. Everyone is incompetent. Everyone is a joke. Everyone is a disappointment. Because the one perfect thing in her life is gone. He is dead, and he is never coming back.

Ophelia reaches out to grab his pant leg. She remembers buying him these pants at Bloomingdale's. He looks so sharp in them. She tugs on the fabric, trying to garner his attention.

Finally, it works.

He looks down and sees her, and a small smirk falls across his face.

Austin can see her.

And save her. Praise God.

He raises his opposite leg, and all that Ophelia can see is the leather loafer she got him from Cole Haan hovering over her.

"Oh look, a bug," Austin says, with the same casual tone he'd use to comment on the weather.

The shadow of his shoe blots out the light as it descends.

Ophelia's scream is cut short as the polished leather crushes down, the pressure forcing her organs to burst through her exoskeleton with an explosion of agony.

Her consciousness lingers just long enough to feel her body crack and splinter beneath the weight of the man she loved, as her insides spread across the marble floor like jam on toast.

And then everything fades to black.

CHAPTER 13

Her head cracks like an eggshell under a boot heel. Pain flares between her eyebrows as if a drill is burrowing into her skull, the high-pitched whine drowning her screams. Blood and brain matter splatter in a grotesque Jackson Pollock of gray and crimson across the pristine walls.

Is that what getting squished like a bug feels like? Your insides spilling out of you like glue squeezing through the little orange tip of the bottle? Your organs reduced to nothing more than colorful paste on the bottom of someone's shoe?

The pressure builds until your exoskeleton gives way with a sickening pop, your once-complex body now nothing but a smear of what used to be life. Each nerve ending screams its final message as consciousness collapses into darkness, your entire existence reduced to a stain someone might wipe away without a second thought.

She wants to scream, but all she sees is darkness.

Her sense of smell is gone.

But her hearing is... it's there.

It starts with a small hum.

A low vibration, so low she can barely hear it. And then she feels it. A buzzing by her side.

She can't quite figure out what it is. The pain. It's her head, or what's left of it. It's throbbing with big, heavy breaths, like the tick-tock of an old grandfather clock. Tick-tock. Tick-tock.

But then she hears it, clear as day.

The ring of a telephone.

Can she do it?

Can she will herself to open her eyes, or whatever is left of them?

Before she knows it, her eyes are open, stung by the brightness of light pouring in from the floor-to-ceiling windows. She turns her head to the left and sees a buzzing phone dancing on the white bed sheets.

It's her phone.

On the bed of the Presidential Suite.

She looks down at her hands, human. Not bruised or broken or crushed by the foot of her late husband. And her legs, she can move them. The pain in her hip is gone. She lifts both of her legs in the air, kicking them with a delightful fury.

Her heart flutters.

She's alive.

She's here!

Ophelia turns over and picks up her phone. It's Liberty calling. Libby , that is! Her Libby.

She answers the call and puts it up to her ear as her head spins. The liquor, it's building in her stomach, sloshing and rolling around. Her head pounds, she needs water. ASAP.

"Mom?" Libby says.

A tear begins to fall from Ophelia's eye, and then a few more. Soon, tears are streaming down her face and onto her ruffed-up robe.

"Hi, Libby," Ophelia says as her voice shakes.

"Mom, I tried to call you last night, but you didn't answer. You were supposed to call me before you got to the hotel."

Ophelia wipes the tears away from her eyes and pushes her sandy gray hair behind her ear. "I'm sorry, Libby. I am so sorry. I had a few too many glasses of wine, and I just forgot."

Silence fills the air.

"Libby, are you there?"

A sigh breathes through the phone. "You've been forgetting a lot lately."

Ophelia shifts in the bed as her heart begins to beat faster in her chest. "You're right."

"It's okay, you know," Libby says. "It will all be okay, Mom. I love you."

Pressure builds in her chest as tears well in her eyes. "You do?"

"Of course I do. I'm so grateful for everything you've done for me."

"But I've been, I've been horrible to you lately," Ophelia cries. She's bawling again, and tears rush down her face like a waterfall. "I've been critical of everything and everyone. Your life choices, your career path, even that goddamn shirt you were wearing on that picture of you on Instagram. It was too small, but I shouldn't be that critical. I'm sorry. I'm sorry for everything. I love you. I love you for who you are. And I want you to be happy. And I want to be with you and support you through this journey of yours. And I don't ever want to miss a moment of it ever again."

When Ophelia finally hangs up the phone, she sits on the edge of the king-sized bed, staring at her reflection in the mirror on the opposite wall. She looks frightful. Her sandy silver hair sticks out in all directions, mascara runs down her cheeks from the tears, and the white hotel robe is wrinkled and stained with what seems to be red wine. She looks like a wreck, nothing like Ophelia Augustus of Decatur who moved through life with her chin up. Nothing like the woman who would look down her nose at anyone who dared serve her the wrong scotch.

She rises from the bed, her legs still a bit shaky, and walks over to the welcome basket that still sits perfectly on the round wooden table. She picks up the bottle of Bordeaux. There's maybe a glass left, but she quickly pours it into the sink. The deep red wine swirls down the drain like blood.

Ophelia watches it disappear. She catches sight of herself in the bathroom mirror and holds her own gaze for a long moment.

"Get yourself together, Ophelia," she whispers.

She reaches for her phone and opens her *Hotel Finder* app. Her thumbs hover over her draft review of the St. Simon, with its petty complaints and exaggerated grievances.

She deletes it all and types five simple words: Changed my life. Highly recommend.

She pauses, looking around the room that had terrified her just hours before. Maybe room 777 isn't haunted by evil at all. Maybe it's haunted by whatever we need most, a mirror for our souls, cruel but necessary. The Presidential Suite hadn't given her luxury; it had given her perspective. And that was worth more than all the Glenfiddich in the world.

Then she checks the time—7:42 AM. Libby's graduation isn't until noon. She can make it if she hurries.

Ophelia rushes to the shower, suddenly energized with purpose. For once, she isn't concerned about the water pressure or the temperature of the room service coffee she'll order. There's a daughter waiting for her across town, and this time, she'll be there with nothing but love to give her.

AUTHOR'S NOTE

Thank you so much for reading *Motel St. Simon*. If you enjoyed your stay at the St. Simon, you might also like my first novella, *The Presidential Suite*, which takes place in the same hotel. It's available in print and ebook on Amazon.

If you were intrigued by the story of Ophelia Augustus—she'll be back *very* soon. Her daughter, Libby, has just accepted a precarious and fascinating new position at a company in upstate New York called Corporate Solutions Incorporated, and things take a strange turn after an unexpected promotion. Keep an eye out for *Compliance*—a full-length horror novel that follows Libby's journey, coming soon.

To stay updated on all new releases, follow me on Instagram: @ev.dean.

Also, in this copy of *Motel St. Simon*, I've included the first chapter of my novella *Spores*. It's my personal favorite piece so far—I hope you enjoy this sneak peek at Chapter One.

A SNEAK PEEK OF SPORES – NOW AVAILABLE ON AMAZON BY E.V. DEAN

CHAPTER 1

When I arrived in Baton Rouge, everyone made it a point to tell me that something strange was happening in this small city nestled in the darkest part of the Deep South.

"The sun hasn't come out in months," the janitor at the airport told me. "I've lived here for thirty years and I ain't eva seen nothin' like that."

"It's so dang hot that I just saw a hound dog chasing a rabbit—and they were both walking!" cried the bartender. After I left the airport bar, I noticed that the temperature on the thermometer outside reads at 112 degrees—*without the heat of the sun*. The air was thick and heavy with a faint metallic aftertaste.

"Animals been goin' missin' out here," explained the waitress at dinner. "I just lost my pit bull last week. He just up and dipped. Never came back. Saw him outside chewin' on one of them yellow things and then he just took off."

"I've never seen a summer this odd," explains the wise and wispy professor. We sit across from each other at a small coffee shop by the university. He clutches his cup of iced coffee with worn and wrinkly hands. His short white hair falls just over the top of his forehead, showing the deep wrinkle in his brow. "I've been teaching here for years and I have never seen a summer without the sun. Crime has been up. It's been so muggy that even now my house is beginning to mold."

That was the main concern of the city of Baton Rouge. The high humidity was causing an unusual amount of fungus to grow. The entire quad of Louisiana State University was speckled with the birth of bright yellow mushrooms. No matter how many times a landscaper plucked the little fuckers, they popped right up in the same spot the next day. In fact, grooming the shrooms appeared to make the problem even worse—they got bigger and bigger, with thick tendrils that dug into the ground. If you picked a small mushroom one afternoon, it was very likely that the next morning you'd find an even bigger one in its place. Maybe you'd even find a dozen new spores.

Nature was not taking their removal kindly.

"I think when they use their equipment to remove them, they are actually spreading the stuff even further," the old man says, letting out a deep sigh. His breath smells like peppermint and coffee with just a hint of last night's whiskey.

Professor Gregory Brighton had begged me to come down to LSU from Columbia to explore what was happening in this strange city.

"Beatrix, I'm so happy you're here." He smiles weakly. His hands tremble as he picks up the napkin from the table and blows his nose into it gently. He sighs deeply and rubs his eyes. They're bloodshot and jaundiced from the increased amount of allergens in the air. "No one wants to really get to the bottom of what's going on. I've called the state, the governor, no one cares. Something bad is happening here. And I think the media is in on it."

"Why do you say that?" I ask.

"Because they keep trying to tell us that those *things* aren't toxic. I don't believe them, I've seen it with my own eyes! I've seen how it changes people the longer they are exposed."

"Well, Dad," I say. "Hopefully I can figure out some way to help."

Like my father, I am a professor but while he studies physics, I study history . . . and the occult. I'm only paid for the former, but the latter is why I am really here. While my father didn't always want to acknowledge my peculiar field of study, he didn't have many options left. His house was slowly becoming consumed by this fungus, and like a stubborn New Yorker, he wasn't planning on leaving Baton Rouge without a solution.

But I am concerned.

How could I not be?

My father lives down here in the strange South all by himself and he refuses to leave. I have to get him out of Louisiana before he gets sick too. My mother passed away a few years ago and I can't bear to see him meet the same fate.

"Hopefully it's nothing," he grumbles. By the furrow of his brow, I can tell he doesn't even believe himself. "Maybe it will be over in a few weeks . . . what do I know?"

My stomach turns. This isn't my father. He's a man of reason and intellect and what is happening here is neither reasonable *nor* intellectual. Something bizarre is happening and the more I talk to people in Baton Rouge, the more irritated I get with their ho-hum complacency for their situation. I grew up in the Northeast and pride myself on being an action taker. I don't wait and sit back and hope for the best. While I like visiting the South, sometimes I can't stand Southern malaise! Where I was raised to tackle problems head-on, I've noticed a tendency here to accept difficulties with a quiet resignation.

My father is getting too complacent.

He lets out a loud sneeze as he shakes. And in that moment, I realize that everyone around me is sneezing or sniffling. Should I wear a mask? Cover my eyes? Take an allergy pill?

How can I keep my father safe if I can't even keep myself safe?

"Beatrix," he says. "I have a student in one of my classes who thinks that he knows where all of this is coming from."

"Really?"

"Yes, his name is Jeremiah. He's a sweet boy from here in town. He told me that there's a spot along the river where all of this is condensed. All of these spores are everywhere—he says it's like a jungle in there of these big heaping fungi. I don't really know what to think. He thinks it's all coming from this spot . . . but I haven't seen it for myself."

"And why is that?"

"Oh, well, you know—it's a bit of a walk off the road in the woods between the road and the river. And it's quite muddy out there given this weather we've been having. You know, my knees don't work so well anymore. I can't go trekking through the swamp like that. Plus, I'm a Yankee. I don't want anything to do with any critters in these woods out here, they are no joke!"

I nod. He has a good point. I'm not too keen on alligators and snakes either. We are New Yorkers to the core. I can handle a big rat and a cockroach, but an alligator is a bit out of the question. Up until my mom passed, I never pictured my father ever living outside the city. Now he was in the Deep South. It was a completely different world.

From what I knew, he was pretty much enjoying his time until things got unsettling.

"I'll connect you with Jeremiah," he says. "He's a sweet boy, a bit odd, but sweet. He can take you to the spot and maybe the two of you can figure out what's causing this mess?"

Do I want to get to the bottom of this strange phenomena? Maybe. Do I want to get my father out of this stinking, rotting, city—absolutely. And I will humor him by any means necessary to make sure I can get him out of Baton Rouge safely.

"Sure," I say. "I'll meet Jeremiah."

If you enjoyed this excerpt of Spores, you can purchase the full version on Amazon or read it in Kindle Unlimited.

EV Dean brings haunting New England folklore to life from the shadows of Los Angeles. A Phillips Exeter alum whose horror fiction walks the knife-edge between reality and nightmare, Dean has cultivated a devoted following with her chilling Bunny Foo Foo series and the acclaimed Darkest Hour novellas. **You can follow EV Dean on Instagram at @ EVDean_author or visit their website at EVDeanWrites. com.**

Made in United States
Orlando, FL
22 May 2025

61503863R00049